BOOKS BY K. M. HERKES

The Stories of the Restoration

Controlled Descent

*Turning the Work**

Flight Plan

*Joining In The Round**

Novices

*collected in paperback as

Weaving In the Ends

Rough Passages

Rough Passages

The Sharp Edge of Yesterday

NOVICES

K. M. HERKES

Print: 978-1-945745-15-7

Ebook: 978-1-945745-16-4

originally published electronically as
Fledglings *and* Fault Lines *in 2014*
Print Edition June 2020

Dawnrigger Publishing, Illinois USA

Cover Art: R. J. Taylor

CONTENTS

NOVICES

1: LEAP OF FAITH

JOE MITANI FELT eyes on him the moment he left the coffee shop with breakfast for himself and his partner. The street was crowded even for the morning rush, more so than when he'd arrived, and some of the loiterers were staring openly. Their looks of apprehension chilled Joe as much as the blast of cold March wind at the café door, and he looked around to see his police escorts moving in.

The small-town atmosphere made any stranger stand out. A tall Asian man with long braided hair was downright exotic, but the edgy ambiance warned him his occupation was probably more of a concern than race; word spread fast in small communities, which meant his observers knew who he was and why he was here. There were drawbacks to working for the Rydder Institute for Analytical Psychiatry and Neopsychology, just as there were undeniable benefits.

Facing the occasional outbreak of hostile prejudice came with the job.

The Institute was professionally regarded as the recovering nation's top psychiatric treatment center, but its public reputation was less favorable. The Institute's close working ties with the Civilian Security Bureau were a mixed blessing when it came to soothing concerns about power and corruption. The media's tendency to spread dramatic myths and promote disinformation for the sake of entertainment was no help at all. What most people believed neopyschs could do had less to do with fact than with fiction. Yes, neo-psychiatry protocols could eradicate the capacity for free will under the proper conditions, but those conditions were not nearly as common as the average citizen believed.

Anonymity was an adequate defense against confrontation in urban areas like Minneapolis where Rydder was based, but it was impossible to go unnoticed in a town like Belleview, which topped out at seven thousand souls. Some of those souls were clearly waiting for Joe to uncover someone's dirty secrets with perceptive skills that mimicked mind-reading. The rest looked concerned that he might wield the persuasive powers that could make the taunt "go jump in a lake" into an undeniable order. He would never indulge in such privacy breaches or coercion —*couldn't* do so outside a tightly proscribed set of circumstances—but mythology was impossible to defeat with logic. The crowd's concerns were rooted in lies, but their fear was real.

Mob aggression was the reason the CSB insisted on assigning protective details to neopsychs on visits like this one. Hypothetically the police presence discouraged potential threats to valued resources. In reality it often made already-nervous people anxious enough to act on those fears.

Joe preferred immersion to isolation. He'd had ample time to get acquainted with the two uniformed officers dogging his footsteps. They'd been with him since his arrival in town the previous evening. Now was as good a time as any to enlist them in a little public education effort. As they herded him past the trending-angry bystanders, he turned to the one on his left. "So, Fergus, you've had an Institute course or two, right? Which ones did you take? How do you like the results?"

He pitched his voice to carry to all the assorted eavesdroppers. Fergus caught the conversational ball with a smile and answered in an assertively cheerful tone. "I like them fine. I've had the anti-addiction workup and a crisis response package that includes negotiation techniques. Mike, too. We're better cops for it. Ask anybody on the force—well, anybody except Ginny in Dispatch. She hates arguing with me now. Sometimes I win."

The nascent tension dissipated on a ripple of laughter. Fergus and his partner had taken courses on crowd management, too. Soon Joe was fielding direct questions from curious onlookers. He had to tune out subdued snickering from his earbug while he did so, which meant he'd fulfilled the original purpose for the jaunt as well. None of the sensitive electronics had degraded since their last use. His pin camera and the two-way scrambled radio feed were both working perfectly.

It was a cold, busy walk back to the hotel, but not a long one, and the destination was impossible to miss. The tiny business district was heavy on agricultural supply and services, and at six stories the Belleview Center was the tallest building in town. The historic multi-use structure also housed the county CSB headquarters and boasted the town's only fine dining establishment.

Today the picturesque frontage was decorated with tubs of early bulbs in bloom, and the seating group in the first-floor atrium was occupied by a gaggle of teenaged girls pretending to study. Once indoors Joe said, "I'm being tailed, Kalyani. See him?"

His partner laughed, four flights upstairs in their temporary observation room, and her rich Gulf State accent rolled through the tiny earbug speaker. "Y'all think I've gone blind? Of course I see him. One-twenty from your heading, scrawny teen male, fidgety as a frog on a hot plate. Why are you asking? Feeling threatened by him?"

"Hardly." The boy lurking outside the front doors couldn't weigh more than forty kilos. "He caught my eye, that's all."

Joe's stalker had tangled hair and the puppyish build of early adolescence, and his skin was almost the same warm-brown shade as his hair. At this latitude and time of year, that marked him as a rare multiracial exception to Belleview's white homogeneity. The boy's expression was equally interesting. Sorrow and resignation were a surface mist over angry fear.

His face was child-rounded and shone with good health, but he carried deep scars on the inside. It was a look Joe saw all the time on much older faces—even in the mirror, after bad nights—but it was unusual to see it on one so young in a sheltered community like this one. The world which had shaped this boy was far from the anarchy Joe had known at the same age.

This fresh youngster hadn't been a helpless witness to violence that destroyed lives and homes by the tens and hundreds of thousands. The riots, famines, plagues, and barbarism had ended far too long ago to be personal memories. He was too young to have known anything but the new order, but still—he knew what chaos and loss looked like, and he dreamed of violence and blood. Joe could see that as clear as day

He spoke to Kalyani again. "That's the adopted brother, isn't it? He wasn't home when I visited. He's grown since the image in the profile, but he's distinctive."

"That's Eddie, yes. He tagged along with our prospective recruit, and the clique of pretty young things followed them both. Captain Reston chased the boy outside but not the girls. Interesting social web here, loads of suppressed hostility. He's up here now—Reston, I mean—chatting with the best-and-brightest. Friend of the family, it seems."

"And how is our prospective recruit doing?"

"Anxious. I pegged his fitness at 'big doubtful' on arrival. That's going to drop to 'damned unlikely' if he hits the nervous-tension thresholds within ten minutes. I'm betting he will."

Back upstairs in the side bedroom of the hotel's largest suite, Joe set down Kalyani's coffee and gave her black ponytail an affectionate tug. She rolled her eyes at the stocky gray-haired man standing near her workstation. *He's all right,* that look said.

The police chief shook Joe's hand in greeting. "I just stopped by to say good luck to Acey. Getting that letter-of-interest made his Dad real proud, let me tell you. Some of us know who the good guys are. Oh, and that thing you did, on your walk? As good as a month of PR work on funding more training. Thanks."

"No, thank you. For this." Kalyani waved at her console and the wiring. "Certified-clean electronics, modern cable runs, and stable electricity 24-7? We're lucky to find any one of those, most places under pop ten-k. Y'all are rebuilding a good town here. Good people."

One of those good people had called Kalyani a towelhead when she got off the train yesterday. Good wasn't perfect, and Captain Reston's expression said he knew it.

"We are the county seat," he said. "We're up to thirty thousand residents now, and we try to be a good example. You can thank AJ for the tech. Acey's dad, that is. Alan Senior. He blew the city budget funding chip-rot recovery after his Restoration appointment. I thought he'd blown his chances for election too, but we made a fortune. For three years we had the only clean data storage in the tri-county area."

Kalyani's console emitted a ping. "Sorry, Joe. That's your cue."

Joe gestured to the hall door, "If you don't mind, Captain. Looks like it's back to work for both of us. Privacy guidelines. Please don't get your hopes up. We do these evaluations in the field for a number of reasons, but the failure rate is part of it."

Reston's frown was thoughtful. "I'd best roust Ace's fan club, then. Last thing he'll need is an audience to disappointment. We'll try to keep his pesky shadow out of your hair too. I do miss the days before individualized education and free-study days. Life sure was a lot easier for the adults back when the troublemakers were locked up in classrooms all day."

Once he'd left Kalyani said, "What's his issue with Eddie, I wonder? The boy has obvious emotional issues, but I didn't get a rebel vibe off him."

"He has a social record of outbursts and fighting. Law enforcement tends to frown on that."

"Because he gets bullied, I bet, not because he's defiant. There's not a whiff of conflict between him and the best-and-brightest. They're like a pair of shoes. What was the home visit like? I'm still jealous that you got a home-cooked dinner out of this trip, by the way."

"No, you aren't. You got to play with computers all evening. It was an awkward meal. The parents carefully made sure I knew Eddie came from the county Restoration foster home. In case I thought juvenile delinquency was a genetic flaw, I suspect."

"Ah, family drama. Nothing like it. I should use this as an example next time someone challenges the need for these natural-environment assessments. Presumptive profile tells us one thing, twenty-four hours on-site refutes it all."

"You really don't like him?"

"Acey? I like him. He's a sweet kid. But he's nothing special. Oh, well. Better to we spot the flaws before we start than destroy their minds later."

"And every dataset we bring back helps refine the selection process," Joe piously finished the quote from their boss's annual lecture. "Doesn't make it any easier to play the villain. Some egos need deflating, but this one—if his profile is solid, then he's made of raw sugar. If his profile is The bad news is going to melt him."

The drill was getting old at this point in Joe's tour of duty. He made a fitness judgment, Kalyani confirmed it with hard data and—in all but one of the forty cases they'd evaluated in the past nine months—the news would be bad. The best they could do was to deliver crushing disappointment with sensitivity. It hurt. The good they accomplished by polishing the Institute's public image wasn't much of a consolation prize.

Kalyani looked up, assessing him with warm and loving sympathy. "Be strong, big boy. He's young, he'll heal. Let's get it done."

Joe got going. At the sound of the door opening, the tall young man standing by the window turned fast with relief shining on his face. "I was beginning to think maybe you'd forgotten about me," he said.

"Of course not." Joe extended a hand. "I'm Dr. Joji Mitani. You're Alan Jenson, right? Let's take care of the legalities first. This session's being recorded, and the contract your parents signed last night allows me and my partner build a full psychological profile on you. You're consenting as well, yes."

"I know. I mean, no, or yes, I'm...um." Alan ground to a halt.

His face was flushed, his handshake loose and a little damp. Joe noted those details, then took a sideways step inside his head and mentally shrugged into his professional shell. Faster than thought, he absorbed a thousand more barely perceivable cues of micro-expression, body language and scent. Every neopsych had a uniquely personal way of internalizing the imprinted skills and conditioning that made them so dramatically effective; Joe's choice was to dissociate self from skill.

Incompatible, whispered the little voice in his head.

Alan's voice broke half an octave lower when he said, "Look, can you call me Ace or Carl, please? I always look around for my Dad when people call me Alan. And sorry, I babble when I'm nervous."

"That's all right. Call me Joe, then. We're not big on formality at Rydder, and for today this little piece of Ohio is Institute property."

"Really? It looks like the suite my cousin rented for his graduation party." Carl blushed bright pink. "Bad joke, sorry. I know what you meant. You meant legally. I passed civics. Obviously. And I'm babbling again."

Anxious, excited and insecure: all perfectly normal reactions for a fifteen-year-old boy. Pale blond like his mother, likely to be even bigger than his burly father once he pushed through puberty, right now he was all elbows and knees and awkward angles. The deep blue eyes were direct and clear. He seemed like a nice kid.

And that analytical voice in Joe's head whispered: *unsuitable*.

The rest of the next two days of interviews would only be window dressing, or as Kalyani liked to call it, "putting drapes on the casket." Despite the outstanding test scores which had attracted the Institute's attention, this was just a bright, normal boy; a well-fed, well-adjusted advertisement for the new social contracts still being hammered into place by the fledgling government of the Restored United States.

Joe waved to the seating area. "Have a seat. Let's talk

about your Secondary finals. You blazed through them in the top percentile a full year early. Impressive work."

Carl stayed at the window, not the normal response of a bright young man being given a chance to brag. He gazed outside at flat brown fields. "Stupid tests. I guess I should've sabotaged my scores like I did last year, but I didn't expect a recruiter. I thought applying and waiting for the answer would give us enough time. Do you ever allow delayed admission?"

His voice cracked high again halfway through the question. At the same time, a horde of minor physical changes pushed the intensity of his still-maturing personality from mundane to phenomenal with an abruptness that left Joe dizzy. *Not so normal after all.*

"Jay-sus," Kalyani said. "Every index jumped fifteen points or more, without even an elevated blink rate. That's an incredible job of masking. And if I didn't know better I'd say he shucked the regular-kid suit because he sensed you were ready to let him down easy. Which means he's as perceptive as all get-out too."

Joe thought the same, and he moved to a seat on the couch. "All right, Carl, you have my attention. Keep talking."

"About what?" Carl asked warily.

Good. Wariness means he's smart. "Start with the cheating claim." Joe kept his voice level, kept his excitement inside. This boy had talent. "Why would you deliberately blow your mastery exams to avoid recruiters from Tertiary programs? And why stop?"

Carl leaned back against the window glass. It made his face hard to see against the cloudy sky behind him, and he folded both arms across his chest. "You know Ohio's an Option state, right? You know what that means?"

The oblique questions set Kalyani into a distracting fit of giggles. "Sorry," she said when Joe glared at one of the cameras. "But how often do you see decent evasion posturing in a kid his age? It's like watching a lion cub try to drag home an elephant by the tail. Ridiculous but adorable."

Joe decided to see where the evasion led by going into patient lecture mode. "Yes, I know Ohio's one of ten territories that offers adult emancipation to minors as far as seven years under the Fed line. Applicants have to complete the process unassisted, government service obligation can be immediate or deferred. What's the point—ah." His memory offered up a relevant tidbit of trivia. "I think I see where you're going. Your brother turns thirteen in the fall."

"Exactly. The plan was to get him straight into the Forces, but he isn't ready yet. He needs at least another year or two. I could've stalled off my parents about applying for an internship for a few months, maybe even until next spring. We could've done more practicing. But now... I can't leave him here alone here. He won't last—people don't—"

Joe raised a hand to stop the babbling. "You seem certain that Institute will want you in the first place. This is only an assessment, remember. You might have all the time in the world."

"Fine. Skip the razzle-dazzle and assess me." Carl moved to the chair across from Joe with slumped shoulders and scuffing feet, and he dropped into the soft seat with a graceless thud. His feelings were written harsh across his face; the blue gaze remained steady even as his jaw went tight with the effort of holding the eye contact under Joe's focused attention.

He was maintaining a level of emotional exposure most people couldn't manage without training, and doing it in front of a neopsych was the psychological equivalent of stripping naked. Joe's breath left his lungs in a surprised cough as he adjusted to the flood of sensory input. The boy's determination was staggering.

Carl had good reason to be confident he would be accepted.

Kalyani sighed. "If his psyche was any more grounded we'd need a shovel to get under it. I know we have to run all the exams, but with these numbers we'll be flayed if we don't pull him into the program. If his sib needs a year—or two or five—we can wait, right? We've never done it, but that doesn't mean we can't."

Joe considered the fear he'd seen under the belligerence in Eddie's expression. Ohio was not only a option state, it was also a bastion of historic social values that fed social problems like familial abuse and institutional denial. He said, "Kalyani, take a radio and track down the brother, please." Then he told Carl, "Before I decide, I'll need to see you together."

Carl took a deep breath. "Eddie's on the fire stairs one floor up. Tell him you're bringing him to me, or he'll run." His voice developed an edge. "If you're thinking we're more than fosters and friends, it isn't like that. I like girls fine."

With that one statement Joe was reminded of all the insecurities and embarrassments of being fifteen—and all the confusion having the kind of sexual identity many neopsychs had could bring into a teen's life.

He said with amusement, "I couldn't care less what trips your trigger, Carl. I can see it isn't Eddie. What I *don't* know is what Eddie wants for his future, and I want that answer straight from him, not from you. Are you sure he's in the building?"

"He's where I said." Carl inhaled slowly, then let it out hard. *Trusting. Bracing for trust to be betrayed.* "Eddie's different. That's the problem. People don't do real well with different here. He always finds me. I always know."

Kalyani herded Eddie through the door a couple of minutes later. The younger boy ran across the room and flung both arms around Carl hard enough to rock him back on his heels. *Love, pride, ferocious worry*; those were the impressions that slammed into Joe's senses.

Eddie was the dominant one in the pairing, which was unexpected but made sense the more Joe saw of Carl's temperament. At its core was a drive to comfort. He was a fixer, not a fighter.

Joe watched them steady each other, looked up to Carl's eyes, saw despair and wistful regret mingling there. If forced to the decision he would turn his back on his own future to stay where he felt he was needed now.

That, more than anything else, fed Joe's resolve to find a better solution.

He gave Eddie a long careful look. The boy turned inside the circle of Carl's arms and gave back as good as he got in the staring department for a second before his gaze skittered away. The hazel eyes conveyed a sense of distance, as if he watched things no one else saw, and he was jiggling one leg, burning off tension. He radiated *tough*, with an edge of defiance that was no doubt the source of the police captain's annoyance.

Analysis kicked in. Abused, but not recently; the damage deeply integrated, external support stabilizing the irrevocably-altered emotional foundation. Trust would never come easily, nor attachment, but the foundations for them were slowly being built, and the aggression should stabilize within tolerances.

Should. If he got a chance to mature and master self-control. Remove the external support at this point, and the debris of old trauma would crush that underdeveloped sense of self. Joe asked, "Eddie, what do you think is going to happen if Alan—sorry, Carl—moves away for a Tertiary program and leaves you behind?"

Eddie looked down and took his time gathering his thoughts before answering. *Translating.* Cognitive processing well off verbal norms, compensations well-rooted and functional. Happier working with his hands, with anything physical, than with words.

"Get mad, hurt someone," he said. "Jail, probably. I can't do the army forms right on my own yet. Chief Reston calls me punk, Mom says I like hitting too much, and people poke me. They like making me go off, and I can't stop. I try. I do."

He had intelligence—his statement showed that—but no sophistication, no depth of awareness. Time was the only cure for childhood, and Eddie would never get a chance to grow into himself if he remained where pressure from every side forced him into a mold of low expectations.

Different. An idea formed on that word. Joe looked to Carl. "How did you know where he was hiding?"

"We always know." Carl shrugged a shoulder. "More him than me."

Eddie's face lit up. "I'm really good at hide and seek."

"Good." Joe turned to Kalyani. "Take him somewhere in the building, please. I want to test a theory. Make sure you pick the spot, not him."

Kalyani threw him an exasperated look and took Eddie into the hall. Once they were out of sight, Joe took Carl elsewhere, and they waited.

A short time after that Kalyani radioed. "Okay, give it a go."

Joe said, "Here's your chance, Carl. Where are they?"

"Maid's closet, top floor," Carl said promptly.

Kalyani made a rude noise. "Right."

Joe smiled. "Excellent. Now ask him where Carl is."

After a long pause marked by murmurs Kalyani said, "You're hoping to tempt Esoterics with them, aren't you? It sounds like the parents would've signed a release for Eddie."

Would. Her word choice wasn't encouraging. "But?"

"Esoteric Research already has plenty of intermittent, unreliable psychic phenomena to study, and he says Carl's in a tiny box full of boots and guns. Insists on it. Sorry, Joe."

"Don't be." Joe looked around the equipment locker outside Chief Reston's office. Carl was sitting tense and unhappy on the floor. Joe grinned at him and said to Kalyani, "We'll run a few more tests to be sure, but I think things are going to work out just fine."

2: BETRAYAL OF TRUST

THE DOOR to room 308 in the extended-visitation quarters rattled under Joe Mitani's fist. His mood began to slide towards panic when no one responded to the noise. Eddie Jenson ought to be in bed at this hour, and according to the sign-out log, no one had left the dorm all night. Joe pounded harder on the door and wished he'd been awake enough to demand a spare key while he was at the lobby desk. One missing person was disaster enough. Two would be a catastrophe.

A man with ruffled gray hair stuck his head around the edge of door 310. The nameplate by his door identified him as Dr. Jorge Ramirez. He said, "It's holy-crap o'clock in the morning. Do you have to wake the whole building? If you want the weird kid, he's in the center quad doing PT with the fuzzies. Five to seven every single day, the maniacs."

His look assigned Joe to the same lunatic category as the Civilian Security Bureau recruits exercising in the muggy June heat, and he slammed his door. Joe shoved both hands through his hair and pulled back the length that he hadn't had time to braid since his boss rousted him out of bed. Then he pulled his ID from the pocket of his sweatpants and knocked on 310.

"Go away or I'm calling security," Ramirez called from inside.

"Please do. I need to talk to the duty officer."

"You what?" The door opened a crack, revealing one bleary brown eye, a slice of lined, weathered face, and half an angry frown. The man's annoyance cooled to respect at the sight of Joe's ID. Institute Administration rank had that effect on paying students like this man.

Ramirez sighed. "Come on in. I'll even loan you a comb."

The security officer opened 308 for Joe and confirmed that Eddie was in the yard with the CSB academy graduates who were here to undergo security clearance conditioning. That was one crisis averted; Joe only had one lost sheep to locate, not two. He requested that Eddie be sent up on the pretext of a family emergency. It was even true, in a way.

The room was orderly and clean. Rocks and feathers on the desk and frames filled with family pictures were the only personal touches. The austerity wasn't what Joe had expected, but over a year had passed since he'd last seen Eddie, and children changed.

The young man who arrived at a run two minutes later was another unexpected sight. His hazel eyes were still a little *off*, his body language still energetic and aggressive, but the body itself was more than twenty centimeters taller than

Joe remembered, and thin muscle over longer bones made him look a lot more wolfish than puppy-like.

"Good God, you've grown." Joe raised a hand. "Sorry, never mind. That's not important. We need to talk."

Eddie kicked the door shut behind himself. His hair was clipped short, and beard fuzz shadowed his upper lip. He wore only trainers and sweat-stained shorts, and he held a tee shirt in one clenched fist.

"What happened?" he asked in a high, hoarse voice. "Is it Mom? Bernie? Carl?"

Joe's hopes withered at the last question. "Damn. I was really hoping you knew something was wrong already—Carl's gone AWOL, and we need to find him fast."

The sooner they found Carl, the less time he would have to hurt himself or someone else. That he *would* hurt someone was a probability Joe had to accept. This was far from the first time that an intern had gone over the Institute walls. No matter how thoroughly science came to understand the human brain, the mind wasn't always predictable. Some-times all the safety nets failed and a trainee succumbed to psychosis or major depression or paranoid delusion.

And right now, against all calculation, signs pointed to Carl being one of those failures. "Can you tell where he is now?"

Eddie sat on the bed and wrapped his arms around himself, and the guilt in his body language wailed, *I didn't know he was in trouble.* Soon he whispered. "South-south-east a ways. Shit, he's angry."

"You didn't know? I thought you two always knew where the other one was."

That anguished silence dragged on while Eddie rubbed a

hand over his head and collected more words. "I don't always tune in," he said. "I butted out for the heavy stuff. I missed it. He went and left the campus? Without asking?"

Without me? was the plaintive undertone.

"Yes, he did, and that's expressly forbidden at this stage of his training. He might not be thinking clearly, either."

There were good reasons for the public to be leery of neopsychs. Anyone old enough to remember the country before Restoration remembered that their skills hadn't originally been developed for healing. Neopsychs were originally designed as spies and human weapons, and the chains of conditioning that made voluntary oaths against harm into binding ones couldn't be forged until there was a solid base for them.

Interns were sequestered because building that foundation was a potentially hazardous process for bystanders. Even at this early stage, Carl had the power to walk into a crowded store or bank, observe for a few minutes, make a few pointed commands and start a bloodbath. He could walk down a busy street, pick targets, and leave a wave of suicides in his wake.

And if he'd gone off the deep end of sanity, he might consider those actions or worse ones reasonable. Joe said, "I know your contract with Research required the security workup, and that's the barest taste of what he's been going through. Heavy doesn't cover it. What do you mean by 'butting out?'"

Eddie's shrug was ambiguous. "It's hard on him. That's hard on me. Someone complained to Dr. Garam, and he said to butt out or ruin Carl's chances." *Is this my fault?*

"Not your fault," Joe said, inadvertently answering the

implied question. If Carl had become unstable because he'd been deprived of an essential emotional support, then Admin would be having serious words with one Dr. Garam from Esoterics Research. "Right now, I need to know if you can help us bring him back."

Eddie shook his head with slow emphasis—confusion, not refusal. The room phone buzzed. Joe grabbed it and hit the speaker button. "Where do we stand?"

Kalyani said, "We get forty-eight hours unless he shakes someone down in the open first. He's cracked, that's certain; he took down the dorm guards and then the front gate guards the same way. Verbally and non-violently, thank goodness. No sign after that, which is good. BOLO-but-do-not-detain bulletins are out, reports will get forwarded to Director Prescott. Oh, for the bad old days of GPS tracking and cameras everywhere, right?"

Her voice was loud in the quiet room, and Eddie's eyes brightened with a animosity that raised the hair on Joe's neck. "Carl. Isn't. Cracked."

"Maybe not." Joe held that angry stare, cooled it with hard truth. "But he's broken his sworn word, he's already hammered six people flat with verbal neopsych tricks, and he can do much worse. That's fact. SOP is an all-out manhunt, but the Director is willing to stretch the dumb luck of having a public-outreach team here on leave *and* an ace in the hole—that's you—to keep this under wraps."

"Please be our compass," Kalyani said. "Please help us get him back quiet and safe."

Before someone gets permission to shoot him like a rabid dog. That was a warning Joe couldn't say aloud, a protocol written nowhere in the Institute bylaws but engraved into the minds of every neopsych certified to practice off-campus. If they didn't keep their secrets, someone else would control them. The good of the whole had to take precedence over the welfare of any one part.

"We can't do it without you," Joe said.

Eddie was already on his feet and changing into street clothes.

KALYANI NUDGED JOE'S ELBOW, then tipped her head at the rear of their car. Her long hair swung and tickled over Joe's hand, and he pulled his eyes away from the cleavage showcased by her sundress.

Eddie had fallen sound asleep across the back seat, with his head against one door and his unlaced boots against the other. His camouflage fatigues were covered in crumbs, and the wrappers for five sandwiches lay on the floor.

"So much for my breakfast," Kalyani murmured. "I don't think he even chewed. Impressive growth spurt he's going through."

"Almost-fourteen keeping up with Bureau grads in their twenties? I call it unbelievable." Joe glanced at the clock. Nearly time to stop again.

They checked their bearings every ten minutes. The

heading from their navigator had never changed, nor did the distance. "South-southeast" and "far," was as good as it got. Eddie couldn't convert his sense to map measurements.

That brought Joe's thoughts back to their primary mystery. "I should get started on some research now that it's light outside. I can't believe Carl snapped. We don't always get it right, but a total breakdown—it doesn't add up. Prescott signed over Carl's profile to you, didn't he? And we have the releases from CSB Central?"

The waivers from the CSB's national administration would give them temporary authority to override local police hierarchies as well as interrogate and detain citizens at will. They might need that power to get Carl back without publicity. His clinical profile was a weapon for a different fight: it might give them a glimpse into Carl's state of mind, and it would definitely give them the means to control him once they found him.

Kalyani said, "We're equipped with police action waivers, Carl's takedown triggers and everything else on file for him. I grabbed Eddie's files too, because I am thorough. Oh, and look what else." She dug into the duffel bag at her feet. "It's a mobile phone like in old movies. Lots more secure than the regular radios. Some guy out west whipped up a rot-resistant chipset design." She frowned at the device. "But it only works where I can hook into an existing local network."

"Never fear, those will spread." Joe could just barely remember the lost convenience of instant wireless communication. For Kalyani, ten years younger, the novelty value was more powerful than nostalgia, but both factors would drive demand. "Do you have two phones? Two can be more fun than one for so many things."

That mild innuendo won Joe a kiss on the cheek along with a handset that he slipped into the pocket of his shorts. Kalyani glanced into the back seat again. "He looks so cute asleep."

"But it's time for a check-in." Joe pulled to the side of the road. "Let's all take a breather while we're at it."

Pastures, crops and shelterbelts stretched under a hazy sky heavy with thunderclouds. The warm air smelled of cut grass and manure. Joe bent and rolled his shoulders to pop the cricks in his back while Kalyani chased grasshoppers off the graveled shoulder into the roadside brush.

Eddie roused groggy and surly and stomped in circles around the car to stretch his legs. When he showed no sign of settling after a second full circuit, Kalyani whispered to Joe, "He's as red as a ripe apple. I'll go water a shrub while you give him the 'involuntary erections are a normal part of puberty' speech."

"Not my job." Joe waited silently instead. The boy stopped fidgeting once Kalyani was out of sight. Joe went to perch on the bumper next to him and nudged him with an elbow. "All right, Eddie. Quit squirming and get to work. Where's Carl now?"

"Further than ever." The whisper held ripples of suppressed fear along with residual embarrassment. "Southeast. In a box with boxes. Fast."

"Sounds like he hopped a freight." Joe consulted the map. Four major rail lines. "Damn. Could he be avoiding us on purpose? He knows where you are too, right?"

"Not usually. It's work, for him. He—" Eddie spent a moment searching for words. "He isn't like me, plus he'd shut down, like I butted out. Not looking. Still isn't."

"Fine. Good." There was still a thread of hope, then. If they could get an idea of Carl's destination, they might be able to intercept him before it was too late. "Can you get any hint of where he might be going?"

Eddie raised his chin and gazed at the approaching clouds.

Joe gestured Kalyani to silence when she emerged from the bushes. She moved to Joe's other side and copied Eddie's posture, arms folded under her breasts, head tipped back. On her, the pose was contemplative, even peaceful. Eddie was like a support cable in a high wind: pulled taut and motionless, strained to the limit of endurance.

Time slipped away. After several minutes of baking-hot silence the tension eased, and Eddie's chin dropped to his chest.

"Well?" Joe said.

"Home." There was no hint of uncertainty in the quiet word, but the fear reverberated now, along with a raw sense of betrayal and anger. *He left me behind.* "He's going home."

THE BATTERED couch in the reading lounge squeaked every time Kalyani swung her leg back and forth. She was deep in a whispered phone discussion about following their quarry further than planned. Every few minutes Joe put a hand on Kalyani's thigh because the motion destroyed his ability to concentrate on his reading. A few minutes later it would start up again.

When she kicked him, he gripped her ankle and didn't let go. "Now what?"

Kalyani wiggled the phone. "We're set. Prescott pulled major Fed strings, and all rail traffic through to Indiana is on slowdown. Terrorism drill. And from Madison we'll have real wheels and escorts. We'll get ahead in no time. How's your chore coming along?"

"I've done a quick skim through Carl's clinical profile. No

obvious holes. Session notes, background briefs and home news still to go."

They were taking *where* on faith, Kalyani was in charge of *how*, and Joe was tackling the hardest question: *why?* "Let's hope I dredge up a clue or three before we catch up."

"Let's hope we don't starve." Kalyani put her head on Joe's shoulder. "'Go get food and things,' didn't give Eddie much to work with."

"First, tone down the PDA to Midwest-conservative, please." One of the librarians was glaring. Propriety was one of many slippery concepts in a country of splintered local cultures still coming to terms with the larger idea of 'nation' again. In some places kissing in public would get them applauded. In others it would get them stoned. Better to err on the side of safety. "Second, I was only giving him a distraction, and you know it."

"I do." Kalyani shifted easily into a demure, detached position. "I'm torn between hoping he got the job done and worrying about what he considers edible."

Working with adolescents meant knowing the difference between moods and *moods*. Eddie was in one of the latter. Responsibility for the grocery run would settle those roiling emotions one way or another; whether he chose to channel them into work or rebellion was his choice. Odds were good that he'd spent the last hour sulking instead of shopping. As long as it calmed him down, Joe would be satisfied.

He might've even spent the whole time playing with the phone they'd given him so he could call when he was finished. He'd been as intrigued by the toy as Kalyani was with hers.

In any case, he'd gotten a chance to work off his temper

without an audience, and they'd been able to work undisturbed by fuming. And if he decided to literally walk off the anger or chase after Carl alone, then they could track the phone.

The device in Kalyani's hand chirped—thankfully, not loud enough to garner another glare from the librarian. Kalyani glanced at it and grinned. "Hello, chatterbox."

She angled the screen to Joe. "Look at all those full sentences crammed together."

The note read: *im at the car. you said buy whatever we needed so i got overnight stuff like deodorant too. home is twelve hours away on the map are we going soon?*

It was less than ten hours at the speeds they would be traveling, but Eddie had taken the initiative to check. Like choosing to do more than he'd been asked, it was a welcome and surprising sign of maturity. Another message arrived while Joe was rereading the first.

can i punch him when we find him? it read. *im that mad.*

Joe said thoughtfully, "And hello, respect for authority."

"That's respectful?"

"He asked permission."

GLEANING clues to Carl's state of mind from the available data wasn't a simple task, and a small car traveling at high speeds didn't provide an optimal study environment. Joe didn't make much more progress until the Madison CSB branch assigned them a van, a driver, and a proper protection team. Once everyone settled and Eddie was safely occupied wheedling war stories out of the bored escorts, Joe let his own task completely absorb him.

The profile was clean. Carl had taken to the neopsych training like a seal sliding into the ocean. His counselors were monitoring the mother-hen tendencies that all neos seemed to develop, but overall he'd pulled numbers in the top percentiles. The metrics also confirmed what Joe had seen for himself: loyalty was a core trait, one that made this abrupt disappearance all the more inexplicable.

Public records on the family revealed nothing obvious, nor did the community news. The father was regularly roasted for political decisions, but commentary showed he had broad support, the mother was mentioned in her role as a Social Aid administrator but seldom in a critical fashion, and an adopted younger sister was lauded for assorted childish achievements.

There were also two older sisters by blood whose names seldom appeared in public record. A desire for obscurity was not unusual for children of local icons. Distancing was also a typical response, the path Carl and Eddie had both taken. And yet Carl was heading back home like a spawning salmon now.

Joe dove into Eddie's files from there, mostly to satisfy his curiosity. According to the doctor's commentary, the boy's development was impossible for thirteen but reasonable for fifteen. His guess was that an abandoned and malnourished toddler's age had been low-balled by orphanage staff. Eddie had been assigned a tutor and a therapist shortly after arrival and was on a list for the next intake at the closest Armed Forces base.

The Esoterics Research team wanted to keep him. They could statistically confirm his hide-and-seek ability, but it only worked with people, not things, and only certain people. They were intrigued. Eddie's tutor was being creative with his presentation of course content. The therapist was focusing on anger management and otherwise pleased. One marginal note read: "healthy, hetero and hopeful: hide the women and lock up the booze!

Joe found himself reading that passage over and over. "Oh, damn," he said when he finally got the message from his subconscious. He double-checked Carl's clinical indices, and then returned to the Belleview news to find the item that had been tugging at his intuition. *"Damn."*

Kalyani leaned over the seat to read the article under the header: One Dead One Unharmed After Car Hits Tree. "That's what shook his screws loose? Are you sure? Tragic, but no lack of closure, and they aren't family members or part of an expected social circle. The survivor isn't even in the same age cohort."

"Small towns, everyone knows everyone. If you strip off the whitewash, that's a public lover's quarrel and death with foul play suspected. Maybe an accident. Maybe suicide or murder. Carl erased his message queue. With his family connections, he might've heard details that aren't in the story. Yes, I'm sure."

"But why would he care—" Kalyani blinked. "Oh. The dead one was young enough for a puppy-love, first-love dynamic. All right, say Carl wanted to confront the survivor and get the real story. If he suspected a local cover-up, why didn't he sound the alarm? Even an intern can petition for an CSB Central case review. He could've asked for compassionate leave at the very least. To bolt, to run off like this—that part still makes no sense."

Sense didn't enter into this picture. Many insular community norms were beneficial and supportive. Others were not, and their effects could inflict shearing stress on even the most stable mind. It would've made all the difference to Carl, with nature and upbringing in conflict.

"Not just first love, Kalyani," Joe said gently. "Not where he'sfrom. No one on his training team has been counseling him. No one's been *educating* him. And then he gets slammed with this? With the guilt and grief? I doubt he's had a sensible thought in hours."

He looked at the news blurb again. "Local driver Quentin Farley (20) died on impact. Passenger Seth Margolis (29) of Fountain City walked away without a scratch. The cause of the crash is under investigation. Witnesses place the two in a heated argument earlier at 'The Watering Hole,' a long-time town favorite gathering spot and sponsor of the annual Mayfest."

"Oh, those fools." Kalyani's voice went hard when she caught the inferences. "His clinicians didn't ask, because they've forgotten it matters, and he didn't tell, because he was raised in Ohio, where boys don't fall in love with boys. Except when they do."

Eddie turned around, frowning at them, and the van bumped down the ramp to the Rockford checkpoint station.

EDDIE WAS KICKING his heels against the split rail fence outside the border station when Joe finished yelling at people on the phone inside. Joe walked past him without pausing. "I want lunch. Join me?"

Now was as good a time as any for an uncomfortable conversation, and Joe had lost, when he and Kalyani thumb-wrestled over it. He retreated to a picnic shelter in the neighboring rest area and slipped into analytical mode. Eddie hopped onto the table next to him, put his feet on the bench and went still in a now-familiar way, like a dog coming to point. He was looking south over overgrown fallow fields and buckled wire fences.

South was good; it meant they were pulling even.

Joe pushed sandwiches and drinks towards Eddie, then turned to face the scenery too. The side-by-side arrangement reduced the confrontational vibe that Eddie gave off as naturally as sweat, and Joe leaned back so he could see the boy in his peripheral vision.

I won't cause trouble. Don't send me away. Eddie's posture all but screamed his self-centered interpretation of recent tensions. He hadn't yet touched any of the food he'd purchased hours earlier. Now Joe understood why.

"Go on, eat. No one's angry at you," he said softly. "Kalyani is chewing the ears off Carl's program coordinators, that's all. We asked you to buy it for eating. So, eat."

Eddie started on the food with a speed that indicated ravenous hunger. Best to tackle the topic directly, Joe decided. He kicked out his legs and crossed them. "So. Sex."

The chewing noises stopped. *What about it?* The silence was filled with anxiety and curiosity but not shame. Eddie hadn't been infected with that particular poison, unlike his brother. Joe kept his gaze on the fields. The boy moved, a telling shift of weight. "Not ignorant," Eddie said. "Health courses."

"That's plumbing, not sex. What do you think of Dr. Shah?"

A snort. *Trick question?* "She's nice."

"You mean she's sexually attractive. I happen to agree. Our boss Doug thinks I'm much more appealing."

That got him a sidelong look, and another sandwich died for the cause.

Joe gave him a few minutes to digest the food and the ideas before saying, "Outreach teams are always hetero pairs regardless of their personal sexuality or gender. It gives us a lot of data points. Who do the recruits react to, sexually? Me or Kal. Or both. Or neither."

A long still silence was followed by more chewing. Joe made a small gesture. "So. Unlike your rather assertive orientation and identity, Carl skews right at neutral for both. He likes sex with people. Period. Not news, then?"

This time the snort said, *Duh.* Matter-of-fact. Accepting. It wasn't surprising, given how close the boys were, but Joe had wanted to be certain, given the mess that assumptions had already made. "That's a unusual attitude where you're from. Did he have problems with anyone?"

Federal law protected individual choice, and in some places the fundamentals of sexuality and identity didn't matter any more than being partial to redheads or having a thing for high heels. Belleview wasn't one of those places.

Traditional values, traditional prejudices: Ohio harbored a lot of holdout zones where local practices rendered higher legislation meaningless.

"No one cared, because he could act normal," Eddie said after a silence that dragged. The last word trembled with an anger too complex for Joe to parse through. Eddie added, "He likes girls fine. They like him back. Lots."

"I saw the harem, yes. Not unusual," Joe said. "Emotional bonding will always be the overriding factor for him sexually. All right, so he wasn't harassed. Did he have anyone special? Experimentation is normal even when it's taboo."

Eddie's red-apple blush made a reappearance, and he snarled, "He never touched me. He wouldn't."

"No, of course not." Joe waited until the boy got a better grip on his temper. "That's not what I meant at all. Let me ask something else. What can you tell me about Quentin Farley? I know this isn't easy, but I need to ask private things, to help Carl."

"Quinn isn't—neutral," Eddie said carefully. A bubble of humor touched the last word, an echo of *experiment*. He liked the euphemisms. "The Farleys are back fence neighbors. Big farm. And yeah, okay, he and Carl were—special. Why? What did Quinn do now?"

"He died," Joe said. Eddie's reaction to the news was a sticky blend of antagonism and sympathy, and *how did he hurt Carl* this *time?* had been an undertone before that. Joe said, "Quentin died, and Carl's trainers weren't doing their jobs, so he got hit with a shock that whacked him right on an emotional stress point while his brain was already under a huge amount of biochemical strain."

That vague explanation was the best Joe could do for now. There were still unanswered questions, mainly, *why* had Carl's grief had hit that emotional knot of conflicted sexuality hard enough to loosen his grip on sanity. Those contributing factors remained unknown.

Eddie jumped straight to the point with all the directness of his age. "So it's not Carl's fault he didn't ask for permission to leave or whatever?"

Joe held back a smile. "Or whatever, yes. Unless he does something publicly unwise, he won't be punished."

Eddie swung his feet as he started on the last sandwich, relieved by the news and young enough to think feigned disinterest was a mature response. Joe added, "He'll have to get comfortable with himself if he wants to make it to clinician rank though. The job demands a lot of flexibility."

Eddie inhaled and choked on half-chewed bread. He staggered to the edge of the shelter and stood there laughing and coughing until his knees buckled, then rocked back and forth on his knees snickering.

Meanwhile the rest of the group came straggling out of the station. The uniforms headed to the vehicle, and Kalyani strode up the path with the phone at her ear and a thunderous scowl on her face.

"—no excuse," she was saying. "Were you born under a log? Ohio, you imbecile. Ohio, Texas, Carolina and Kansas, to name four of twenty. There's a bedamned list. Y'all knew his zero point, y'all saw those masking stats. It was your job to look deep enough to find the knots and get him counseling. Yeah, I ratted to Prescott first. Have fun collating Observation reports for the next fifty years with the rest of your team."

She punched disconnect and eyeballed Eddie with disfavor. "He thinks it's a joke?"

Joe shook his head, relieving the angry concern in her eyes. "No, he's not part of the problem. Carl won't lack for support, once we haul his ass out of the fire and screw his head on straight."

Eddie made a gurgling noise and went off again, helplessly giggling.

When Joe finally realized what the boy found so amusing, he had to stifle a chuckle himself. "Flexible?" he asked, testing the theory, and Eddie whimpered. Joe chalked up the renewed assault of mirth to *screwing his head on.*

Eddie looked up, their eyes met, and then they were both laughing.

Kalyani raised both hands in surrender and retreated to the van.

EDDIE'S directional sense kept them on the road until south turned to southwest, then northwest. At that point, their CSB team coordinated with analysts and narrowed the target to a specific cross-country freight. From there, coordinating a rendezvous was a matter of requesting a crew change stop through channels and lying in wait at the siding until the train arrived.

A kilometer-long train would've been hard to search car by car, but it wouldn't be necessary. Around one in the afternoon, around the time the train pulled into a yard to add cars, Eddie had volunteered the news that Carl was *with people now*. He'd joined the engine crew in the front cab.

While waiting in a bunkhouse kept on-site for stranded crew members, Eddie's eyes begged Joe and Kalyani for reassurance even while his hands knotted into fists. Joe had no comfort to give. Carl would know there was trouble waiting here: the CSB truck sitting beside the tracks was obvious. If he talked the crew into skipping the stop—if he'd pushed the crew in any way before this—then there would be no leniency.

Joe didn't realize he'd been holding his breath until the train halted on the siding and put his worst fears to rest. He watched through the window of the staff shed and indulged in a quiet whistle when Carl hopped down from the lead engine behind the trio of engineers.

The difference between a fifteen-year-old with potential and the result of a year's intense coaching, conditioning and study were dramatic. Carl had grown past the gawkiness and put on muscle, and he radiated charm even in grubby jeans and a borrowed shirt that was too small to button up the front. The clean-cut, brawny, blond looks and expressive blue eyes were the perfect accessories for that just-another-guy mask of his.

The mask wasn't up to the task of hiding his feelings from a neopsych, not today. Carl might've started the trek in an irrational state of grief, but he'd long since come to his senses and had hours to contemplate the consequences. He was determined to take responsibility for his lapse, but he was equally certain it meant his life was over. Heartache was beginning to tear him apart all over again.

"Wonder twin powers, activate," Joe said under his breath, and Kalyani snorted. She twined her fingers between Joe's and squeezed—*ready*—and they stepped outside as the crew entered, neatly cutting Carl from the herd.

Kalyani and Joe were nearly even in height and an even closer match in skin and hair color; they could be deliberate about doubling their effect on an audience when they chose, and they chose it now. It took no effort at all to put their bodies in sync far beyond a simple matching of stride. Carl stopped in his tracks, shocked into evaluating the display. That response was already drilled to the level of reflex; he couldn't help reading what their bodies told him.

Forgiven, was the gist of the message. *We're here to care for one of our own in need, nothing more. You are embraced, not judged.*

Two seconds. Four fast heartbeats. That was all it took for Carl to get the point. The mask slipped even further, and his eyes filled with tears. He took one step back, and his hands rose to waist-level, palms down, denying the reprieve.

His emotions were a fractured mess that defied immediate analysis. Cracks of guilt and self-recrimination ran deep, and anger was a wide molten stream that threatened to swallow everything else. Joe slid a glance sidelong, and he felt more than saw Kalyani hesitate as well. Carl was barely holding himself together; a wrong move or a wrong word from either of them would cause the complete breakdown that they had feared from the first.

Eddie broke the impasse. He came between Kalyani and Joe, gently broke their handclasp and slipped between them in a swirl of irritability.

Confusion pushed some of the misery off Carl's face. He evidently hadn't gotten as far as wondering *how* he'd been found.

"Hi," he said, and Eddie socked him in the gut.

Joe pulled Kalyani away. She cast a worried look over one shoulder as the pair started wrestling in the summer-dry grass. "I did give him permission," Joe reminded her. "Let them work it out. We have more calls to make."

3: CRISIS OF CONSCIENCE

THE CCFFEE SHOP was a summer social hotspot. A hodge-podge of outdoor tables under an awning filled the sidewalk outside, and chairs of various vintages were filled with breakfast patrons; field crews on break, late commuters fueling up, students staking out study space. Windows were open to the breeze, and a banner on the awning proclaimed, "REMEMBER AIR CONDITIONING? WE DO! COUNT-DOWN TO THE NEW COOL: 34 DAYS!"

Heads came up as Joe approached with Carl at his shoulder and uniformed officers at their backs. Sympathy predominated on the faces. The funeral was scheduled for tomorrow, and Kalyani had arranged matters as if Carl started this trip the way he should've done, with proper permits and guidance.

She was working on lodging and diplomacy at the Belleview Center now. Their current escorts were from Columbus, where they'd spent the previous night. Refusing local support would require some explaining, given the good relationship they'd previously built. Kalyani was playing up a need for hasty coordination, but the truth was that Carl had vetoed the option.

"Don't let them near me." That was all he'd said since they'd reclaimed him. "Not Uncle Mike's people, and not my parents."

Other than that ultimatum, and other than the reunion tussle with Eddie which had ended in laughter and healthy tears, Carl kept his mask up and his mouth shut.

Joe had hashed over the boy's initial shattered responses with Kalyani, and it hadn't taken long to sketch out probable explanations. None of the theories were pretty. Rather than go trampling around town stirring up trouble—and traumatizing Carl any further—they decided to let him lead them to the truth. Joe was in charge of the oblique approach, and he'd decided to start here.

With Carl's parents.

If the boy wanted to distance himself from his family, then brief public contact was the best option for keeping the peace. It would also give Joe a chance to see what kind of emotional debris the confrontation stirred up, and most importantly, he could see how Carl cleaned up the resulting clutter.

He slid a look at Carl as he opened the cafe door. The boy looked ordinary enough today, in a clean collared shirt and cargo shorts that Joe had donated to the cause. Officers Ben and Tasha crowded close inside, then dropped back to a discreet interval as soon Joe glanced at them.

Tasha winked back at him. *We know our jobs, thanks.*

The Columbus pair was diligent, well-trained and friendly, and Joe ordered coffee for them. He firmly believed the CSB's concerns about physical risks from the public were excessive, but excessive wasn't the same as unfounded. Showing some appreciation for their efforts cost him little and built good will.

The Jensons were seated in one of the open window booths: two mature comfortable people chatting pleasantly with the occupants of neighboring tables indoors and out. Jessica's graying hair was a little mussed, her clothes clean but worn, and her expression attentive and kind. Alan was more polished, both in dress and appearance, and his conversational style was more expansive.

It was all an act. Both the earth-mother and the bluff comrade were polished facades that covered passionate, intelligent, driven personalities. Together they made a powerful team, and it was no surprise that Mayor Jenson pushed this town wherever he wanted to go.

Easy to see why Carl had become adept at hiding his feelings, being raised by two experts of the trade. He'd probably mastered that emotional self-defense trick before he learned to read.

Carl took a shaky breath, and Joe pushed him forward. "Go on, you're the one who wanted to play the *I'm all grown up and independent* card. Get it started. I'll get drinks and join you."

By the time Joe's tea and all the coffees were ready, he'd seen enough to confirm his belief that Carl's parents played a major role in his woes. *If only* was a sharp echo behind every word, every smile, every touch they exchanged, along with *where did we go wrong?*

Either they'd guessed about Carl's sexuality, or he'd been open with them. Joe suspected the latter. The boy had too much integrity for his own good. His parents could no more accept him than they could breathe underwater. They were not only products of a culture that labeled differences abominations, they were leaders in it.

Carl stood his ground in the aisle with a pleasant smile in place, but he was crumbling inside. When love came wrapped in acid reproach, it could break down the strongest stone. Joe cleared his throat as he arrived, offered a brush of body contact that said as clear as speech: *Let me get you out of this.*

He bestowed a smile on the couple in the booth: kindness layered over pity. "My condolences to the family. I understand Quentin was a close friend."

Loading the words with innuendo was petty, but Joe couldn't help himself. Intolerance brought out the intolerance in him. He also enjoyed the startled response from Carl. No one made snide remarks to his parents. Not ever. Joe gave him a nudge: *it's a big wide world out there, and you're moving up in it. Pulling on powerful tails is a job perk.*

His verbal jab landed solidly too, but not with the effect he expected. Alan flushed dark in anger at Joe's mocking tone, not the implication itself. When the man stood up, both Joe and Carl had to move back to accommodate him. Alan had the weight of years that his taller son lacked, and he was willing to use that large body for effect.

He stepped a little too close, deliberately challenging, and his voice was loud enough to be heard by the diners outside.

"They were good friends, yes. Quinn was a bright young man who had just started finding himself, and he will be missed. The whole town is mourning the loss of one of its own."

That was said with a sweeping look across the café. The clear implication was that anyone who wasn't grieving would answer to him personally, with unpleasant consequences. Given the man's underlying feelings, that speech was an astounding concession. It came as no shock to Carl, judging by the sad pride reflected in the boy's eyes.

Alan took his son by the shoulders and looked long and hard at him before saying, "Go talk to Seth Margolis as soon as you get a chance. He could use a sympathetic ear right now."

Jessica spoke up. "He's stuck in custody while Mike investigates the crash, poor man. Do go see him. It'll do you both good."

Alan said even more quietly, "And while you're there you can tell Mike Reston that I'm not afraid to take him down if he doesn't resolve this properly."

Carl shrugged out of his father's grip. "Tell him yourself, Dad. You should've set him straight years ago."

The flash of temper was like a gleam of scales at the surface of deep water, and it slipped away beneath a smile so fast that Alan looked uncertain whether he'd even seen it. Carl turned and held out a hand to his mother. She rose and took it in both of hers.

Revulsion sparred with wistful regret under her smile. The dissonance set Joe's teeth on edge, but he had to admire the effort. Carl wasn't the son Jessica Jenson wanted, but he was hers. Like her husband, she was making every attempt to overcome her own beliefs for Carl's sake.

She said, "You look so tired, poor baby. I'm so, so sorry. Did Eddie come back for the funeral too? He writes to us all the time, but he never says anything about you, and you never…do you see much of each other, still?"

A thread of wariness ran through the questions, but it was ephemeral and snapped before Joe could grasp its source. Carl sighed. "Yes, Eddie came too. He'll drop by tonight to see you and Bernie, I think. I won't. This is hard enough for me like this. I'm sorry, I know I don't keep in touch, I would write, but—"

"No." His mother stopped him with a look. "No excuses, sweetie. You were five the first time you ran away from us. I always knew you'd shake off the dust and never look back someday. It's all right. Just remember I do love you. And bend down so I can give you a kiss."

She laughed when she realized that how far Carl had to bow so that she could reach his forehead, and then her reserve evaporated and she took him into her arms. "Go with God, son," she said quietly.

Carl heaved another sigh as he returned the hug, closed his eyes and pressed his cheek against the top of his mother's head.

He didn't look back when he left.

**9:45 AM Wednesday June 15
downtown Belleview Ohio**

CARL NEEDED to burn off nervous energy after leaving his parents in the gossip pit, so Joe followed him over two blocks and down four, back up and across and down again while the town went through its morning routines around them. Ben and Tasha bracketed them, watchful but unconcerned.

They ended up at the minimalist commuter rail depot, which was little more than a metal roof over a concrete slab. Bolts on the support beams showed where wind-breaks could be installed against heavy weather, but today a hot breeze drifted through.

Carl stood staring across the tracks at a big sprawling building. The Watering Hole stood between two lots with burned-out foundations, a relic of the not-so-long-ago time when the town had been larger. The two CSB officers signaled to Joe before taking up posts out of earshot but with views of all approaches.

Don't sneak away on us, Ben's pointing finger warned, which made Joe wonder which Institute team had been through Columbus most recently and what kind of trouble they'd stirred up.

The object of Carl's interest looked forsaken and dilapidated in the morning sun, with weathered board siding, weeds in the cracked brick patio and ruts in the gravel parking lot. The reek of hot beer and stale grease hung in the humid air.

"It's better at night." Carl settled to the concrete floor of the shelter and stretched out his legs. He picked up a chunk of rock and started scraping it against the edge of the slab. "They do a great Sunday brunch."

After a moment's consideration, Joe crossed to the opposite side of the platform to look at the scenery there. The grinding noise eventually stopped, "What am I supposed to say?" Carl asked. *What am I supposed to feel?* "What do we do now?"

"Don't ask me, I'm only a chaperone." Joe hopped down onto one of the rails. "I'm here to sit on you if you need it, nothing more. The pacify-the-parents visit is done, We can kill time until 2 PM tomorrow however you want."

I can be a friend, if you want. Tell me how I can help. Joe kept his eyes on the horizon and his back to the seething emotional mess behind him. Carl continued his minor vandalism. Puffy clouds built on the horizon, and tendrils of dusty heat and damp cool swirled on the breeze.

"I wish someone had sat on me earlier," Carl said. *Crunch. Scrape.* "Monday I came out of a deep session—" a weak euphemism for neurological procedures involving direct electro-stimulation "—so I was catching up on things and there was a message and I saw. Then I was looking at a metal wall and trying to figure out why the floor was moving…" A long pause and ragged breathing. "Did I hurt anyone?"

"Not permanently." Joe smiled at the memory. "You told every poor soul who got between you and the rail yard to hide somewhere and suck their toes. Brilliant really. Remarkably non-violent."

"Why?" was Carl's next question, after a lapse long enough that the shadows had visibly shortened.

"Why what?" Joe replied. "Why did you snap? I'll leave that to your new Cog team and your Ops therapist to explain. Learning experiences and all that. Why did your friend have to die? Life's a bitch. Sorry to break the bad news."

That got him a bitter laugh, and they each retreated to their own activities again. Joe was thoroughly bored with rail-walking before the grinding stopped once more and Carl said, "I don't have to see Seth, do I? We can wait at the hotel for the funeral until tomorrow, and leave right after?"

"Up to you." Joe took up a position nearby but not too close, where they could watch the bar together. People were hosing down the patio and raking gravel now, putting out tables and chairs. "Do you even know Mr. Margolis? Eddie didn't recognize the name."

"He wouldn't."

Joe let the statement simmer in its own cryptic juices. Carl finally said, "I never met him in person. Quinn met him during gov' service in Columbus. He called me a lot at first when he was lonely—Quinn did. Later just to shoot the shit. He was the only person I could talk to about—"

Carl crashed into a rocky silence and blushed deep pink. Joe said in his blandest voice, "About lusting after boys. Note my lack of shock, also my lack of condemnation. Study it, please. Look at me. Believe it."

He waited, measuring the weight of Carl's stare, feeling the boy's nervousness slowly ease. When he judged the foundation laid, he said, "All right, then. The lesson is this: sex is powerful, wonderful and above all else, complicated. You'll learn. For now, let's say I can see that Quinn was important to you. Take it from there."

"Important." Carl sighed. "He always wanted to be important. He was always dreaming big, talking big. He wanted to change the world someday. He would say exactly what he thought." The silence swelled with poignant sadness. "We—ended, when he left, but I was glad. He called girls squishy. Pushy, needy, manipulative, is how I'd see him now."

From across the vast gulf of maturity between thirteen and sixteen. Joe kept tight control over his tone of voice. Carl would hear a smile. "You swung to girls after he went away?"

"Yeah. Did you know that they don't consider squishy a compliment?"

Joe turned to him. "You told a girl you liked her squishy bits?"

Carl was still blushing. "She forgave me. Eventually."

"If you apologize right, people always will." Joe paused to appreciate the way time could ripen stinging embarrassment to sweet nostalgia. "So," he said in due time. "Quinn. You stayed in contact."

"Yeah, and he was happy. Finally. He ended up working the farm after serving, to save up some money, but Seth stuck it out and waited for him. They were going to move to Pitt, where they could go legal. Quinn worked up a portfolio, had a design job lined up, they were going to try a year's contract and if things worked out, maybe more. Why did this have to happen?"

The nuance rang clear now, and Joe recognized the source of the guilt that pushed Carl over the edge. *Why did they hate him and not me?*

The other facts Carl had shared solidified Joe's darker suspicions about Quentin Farley's death into certainty. One ugly theory explained Carl's guilt, his refusal to work with the local CSB, and his reluctance to offer sympathy despite compassion being central to his nature—it even explained his father's cryptic directive.

"You need to face this," Joe said gently. "We've spotted the lies the same way you did, off a million tiny points you can't consciously explain. I don't know what happened exactly, but I know what's tearing you apart. Say it out loud. Let it be real."

Quentin Farley hadn't died in a car accident. Nor had he been murdered by an angry lover. The man had set out to flaunt his happiness in the faces of people who despised him, and he'd paid for the stunt with his life. He might've even been killed by the people who should've protected him—people Carl had grown up respecting, who were now pinning blame on an innocent man.

Carl's face crumpled up, and a shudder ran through his body before he bent over himself and started to weep. "They *killed* him. How could they do that?"

Rage tainted the sorrow fueling those sobs: rage and a deep, fearful shame. Joe kept his distance from the tangled mess and let Carl cry it out. He understood the fear all too well, understood why Carl was afraid to reach out to anyone involved in Quentin's death. When you carried around a hammer, life was nothing but a box of nails. He was afraid of himself, of what he would do to the guilty.

Joe stood and paced quietly, grieving for a life wasted and more, for the ripples of destruction its passing were still causing.

"You will not hurt anyone," he told Carl. "Set that fear aside. If you step even a millimeter out of line, I will drop you before you can open your mouth. Or else Dr. Shah will do it. The primary drop triggers are rudely physical, so it won't be pleasant either way. She's squishier, for what that's worth, so if she drops you, you'll have a nice, soft landing spot."

The whimsical touch to the reassurance served its purpose. Carl's hiccups ebbed to sniffles. When he'd regained enough composure to wipe his face, Joe said, "Your mother's right. It would do you a world of good to talk about your friend with someone else who cared for him. Here's what I think we should do. We'll take you to the station to see Seth, and while we're there, Kal and I rip that place apart and get to the bottom of this."

Blue eyes, red-rimmed and teary, rose to meet Joe's and looked quickly away. Carl's lower lip trembled. "How?"

"We have CSB federal compliance waivers." It wouldn't take long at all to pry out the facts and bring in outside authority if necessary. Joe pulled Carl to his feet and looked up to meet the boy's eyes. "And I'm in a mood. Let's go."

EDDIE AND KALYANI were waiting in the atrium lobby. Kalyani crossed the room to give Carl a big, friendly hug on arrival. "Carl, darling!"

Her hair swung over her shoulders, tangling in Carl's hands, and the official paperwork she held in her left hand crinkled against his back. Carl's face clouded with puzzlement, but he bent to return the embrace properly.

When Kalyani lifted her chin to whisper in Carl's ear, Joe realized what she was planning. Her expression was broadcasting pure mischief. Joe moved just in time to get between her and everyone else. Carl's legs went out from under him as if they'd been cut off, and Kalyani was easing his weight to the ground when Eddie launched himself at them with an angry, wordless yell.

Joe intercepted him, staggering back before the startled

protection team grabbed the panicked boy by both arms and hauled him off.

Carl laughed, a sound that teetered on the emotional edge between humor and hysteria. It came down on the safe side. Eddie stopped struggling as soon as he heard it, and Kalyani gave Carl's blond hair a tousle as she stood up again.

"Now you can stop fretting," she said. "That's the second-hottest trigger in the set, and it's officially passed a field test. Nasty, huh? Aren't you glad the Director will be the only one with access to your permanent codes?"

She waved to the two officers who still had Eddie in hand. "Y'all can let him loose. Go confab with Gio and Marco, will you? We'll be there in a minute. This should go smoothly, but better to plan for the worst and all that."

Ben and Tasha went to have a consultation with their compatriots, who had stationed themselves near the wide stairs leading to the police station on the lower level.

Carl got to his feet and brushed down his clothes, then put out a hand to fend off a swat from Eddie. Joe marveled at the way they had elevated non-verbal communication to a science.

The pair of them looked at each other—*okay?/yes, okay*—and then Carl shoved the younger boy hard enough to nearly knock him off his feet. *I can take care of myself. Think first, next time.*

Eddie prowled off to join the CSB crew, who opened ranks to include him after a slight hesitation. Like called to like, clearly.

"How did you know?" Carl asked Kalyani. "That I was fretting, I mean."

"Are you kidding?" She handed the waivers to Joe with an

expansive gesture. "We work with the clinical finalists between recruiting trips. If I had a dollar for every time I've seen that *what if I overstep?* look on an intern's face I could take everyone here out to dinner. Speaking of meals, how did your breakfast visit go? Joe didn't say on the phone."

She angled her body towards Joe, hiding her expression from Carl behind a veil of hair, and her eyes were full of a worry that belied her cheery voice. *Did he pass?*

"It went all right, I guess," Carl said.

His answer wasn't the one Kalyani was seeking. Joe gave her a nod. *He did great.* "You should've seen him."

Carl had never considered for an instant planting a seed of change that would grow and choke out his parents' weedy disapproval, even though such a seed would've grown easily, given the fertile, loving soil. A quiet phrase or two would've done the trick, and Joe had given him plenty of opportunity.

The thought hadn't crossed Carl's mind. Joe was sure of it.

Kalyani's smile reached her eyes. "His clinical trials are going to be fun to watch, aren't they?"

They could both retire rich if they had a dollar for every intern who failed that final test of working in a therapeutic setting. Even under constant supervision, the temptation to do more than what had been assigned was tremendously strong, because it was so easy. They could make improvements, ease pain and nurture growth well outside the set limits of treatment. And from *could*, it was an awfully short step to *should*. For the patient's own good, of course.

Ego tripped up the smartest and kindest people, and the penalty for succumbing was inflexible. Washouts would never again use their skills on clients in a clinical setting because they would never be given the required final conditioning that enforced proper conduct. It was a potential death sentence for anyone who underwent it, so it would be murder to inflict on anyone who couldn't pass that final trial.

Anyone who'd gotten that far still had a bright future within the Institute if they wanted one, and most did. They made up the backbone and the majority of the staff, doing analysis that led to treatment, supporting and serving the tiny circle of healers they'd once meant to join. Those who were tried and found wanting found new paths again after they stumbled.

Their falls were still a painful thing to witness.

This particular intern had already passed a harder test, and that was why Joe was going to let him tag along now. He took the waivers from Kalyani, signed them with the pen she'd snagged from the hotel check-in desk and set his thumb to the seals to make them official in his mind. The activation was a tangible sensation, like lock tumblers falling at the pressure of a key.

Free to act.

"Forget trials," he told Kalyani. "He's going to be fun to watch today. Let's do this thing."

THE GLASSED entrance door to the reception area closed behind Joe, and the young man in uniform behind the intake counter looked up. He looked from Joe to Kalyani, lingered there, darted a puzzled glance at Gio and Ben in their uniforms at the rear, and then his eyes rose to Carl.

"Hey, Acey," he said. "Sorry about Quinn."

Sympathy. Discomfort tinged with jealousy. Rookie and proud but unhappy that he'd failed to excel as much as others. Nothing hidden.

Joe dismissed him as inconsequential and led Carl past the counter towards a short hall beyond it. Memory placed the holding area past the patrol bullpen and the investigator's cubicles, across from the interview and briefing rooms.

Behind them, the legs of a stool squeaked. The officer said, "Uh, Acey? You can't—uh, you aren't—"

Joe looked back. "Quiet." The protests stopped. Most people were simple, when push came to shove. Easy to intimidate. Simple to command. Flash hypnosis was no parlor trick in the hands of neopsychs who could wield it like a bludgeon when permitted, under certain specific conditions.

"We'll be taking custody of Seth Margolis, Officer." Kalyani leaned over the counter with the waivers and their other paperwork in hand. She peered at the man's name tag. "Noah Miller. Can you get started on these releases, Noah? Push them to the Captain fast as you can. You can lock up that door there behind us too, thanks. We're shutting you down."

Always the diplomat, Kalyani, with please and thank you and looks on her side. She used intimacy instead of intimidation, but the results were the same. Poor Noah Miller scrambled to be helpful.

The day shift patrol was briefed and out, walking beats or on the road. Three on desk duty, filing and writing, and three stragglers from the graveyard shift chatting near the locker rooms. Captain Reston's corner office was shut, the shades drawn. The patrol sergeant looked up from the duty desk.

Sorrow, frustration, alarm, and after one look at Carl, *guilt.* Joe pointed at the sergeant. "Go sit Dispatch. Alert the Captain if there's a major call. Otherwise handle it without mentioning us. The rest of you—" he gathered the two trios with a gesture. "Dump weapons, head to the briefing room. Now."

Two pocket knives, a belt knife and a small-caliber pistol in an ankle holster hit the desktops along with duty-issue dart guns and stun wands. One of the men shook his head, more resistant than the rest, and his hand strayed towards a holstered sidearm at the hip of his jeans.

And then Carl spoke.

"Give me an excuse, Bill." He loaded his voice with thick scorn and used every inch of lanky height to project menace. "Do what he says, or else."

The sound of him sent a shiver up Joe's spine. "Carl—" He waited, trigger on the tip of his tongue, braced for the worst. Just in case he'd been wrong, because he couldn't help but doubt, listening to that crackling, vicious voice.

Carl took one step forward. "Go."

Bill stripped off the gun and headed after his buddies at the double, but there'd been no manipulative power in that order, only venomous hostility. Carl smiled that wicked smile after him and then turned to Joe. "You said fear would keep them in line easiest. How was that?"

His face was alight with humor and as innocent as a brand-new day.

"Half-right," Joe said. "Do not frighten me, please. I like those shorts I loaned you, and you will piss all over them if I drop you hard. Stay with them and keep them quiet."

Carl nodded and strode away after the patrollers. He swung behind the presentation podium in the briefing room, propped his folded arms on the top and stared at the seated men. "You're sitting here, out of the way, until a short internal investigation is completed. Any questions? Ask me anything."

He was fresh-faced and wholesome, his voice courteous and respectful, but icy rage swam just beneath the rippling bright surface of his challenge. That shiver ran back down Joe's back again. He waited, still on edge.

Analysis said: *stable as bedrock, fused together with hope and trust, not a single drop of true cruelty or spite beneath that bedrock.* His own visceral response insisted otherwise.

Then Kalyani was there, brushing past him with a hand at his waist: *I've got this.*

She shepherded four curious and bemused day-shift investigators and one worried dispatcher into the briefing room, saying, "Take your seats and wait, please."

They gave her no trouble at all. Her warning frown was for Carl. "Be good."

"I'll color inside the lines, I promise." He said it low-voiced, with solemn gravity. Truth resonated in it. "If they don't want to talk, we'll sit here and make eyes at each other until you're done with Uncle Mi—Captain Reston."

Kalyani shut the door and gave him a last frown through the window. *Trusting you. Don't let us down.* He grinned in reply. Kalyani made a face and turned away.

"Is he looking at liaison work?" she asked. "Because he is a natural for interrogation."

"He is a steaming pile of scary," Joe said. "At sixteen. Picture him at twenty."

"You did say he'd be fun." Kalyani slid her arm into his. "We're good to go. He's got them covered, and Ben and Gio will bring Seth out as soon as they take photos and get him mobile."

"Mobile?"

"He was in restraints and sedated. Sedated for pain management, his intake says. Injuries include a seat-belt bruise—passenger side—along with multiple fist and boot prints in private places. Three or four days old."

"Damn. Where was Reston and his precious community spirit in all this?"

"Let's double-team him and find out."

They found Captain Michael Reston inside his office. He was sitting with his elbows braced on the desk, face in his hands. A monitor near the ceiling covered the station interior on split views. Noah Miller sat slumped at the reception desk, the two Columbus officers were taking snapshots of a dazed man whose strong jaw and styled brown hair were a match for Seth Margolis' booking image from the news story, and Carl was watching a white-faced, silent audience.

Kalyani pulled out the visitor's chair and let her sun dress ride up her thighs when she sat down. Joe moved in behind her, hands on her shoulders. Kalyani's hand crept up, and her cold fingers wrapped around his wrist. Matched set, beauty and brawn; a classic that never got old.

"You know why we're here," Joe said.

"I can guess, given that you slammed in with waivers and asked for Seth Margolis." Reston lowered his hands and brought up his chin: weathered strength on the outside, melting shame within. His voice kept defensiveness well-hidden under tones of authority. "Throw your damned Security Bureau muscle around all you want. You won't find criminal misconduct, and you don't scare me."

"Yes, we do." Joe enjoyed the way his voice made Reston quiver and read the reaction with interest. The man was ashamed, but not of his own actions. "We scare you, and we can smell your dirty laundry. We'll find it."

"I said we did nothing criminal, I didn't say this was

clean." The man pushed papers across the desktop and turned his screen so they could view stored imagery. "This is pathetic. You could've just asked. I would've filled you in."

The official report was as far from the public story as sunrise from sunset: superficially similar but fundamentally opposite. The truth was less malevolent than they'd feared too, but no less tragic for having its roots in error instead of intent.

Quentin and Seth had indeed left the bar in a state of feud, but their fight followed a much larger shoving match involving assorted named parties with objections to the local pervert bringing his partner onto their turf.

According to Seth's testimony, he'd been an unwitting participant in the exhibition. Quentin had surprised him with the bar stop. They'd been on their way out of town after a day with the family going over details of the upcoming move. Just a little farewell tour, What could go wrong?

Three patrol units responded to the brawl, restored order and sent everyone on their way without arrests to mar their records. That far it was only sordid and sad with a hopeful thread of official restraint. Then one of the patrol cars followed "the instigators of the brawl" onto the highway, and when the driver "began acting erratically" they responded with flashing lights and aggressive crowding. The results proved deadly. Those involved were suspended from duty for a month, with private reprimands on record.

Kalyani sent the home addresses to Eddie, who was upstairs with the escort team awaiting their marching orders. "These two, they're ours," she said. "As for the rest of it—get started explaining why you framed an innocent to save the reps of two bigots."

"No one meant for this to happen. Yes, we bent the news, so what?" Reston said. "It broke no laws and took heat off my guys. It's part of keeping the peace. We're not perfect, but we're trying. Everyone loses when people get stirred up and cause trouble. We would've dropped the suspicious-death investigation after feelings ran cool, and then we would've gotten Margolis out of town."

Where he should've stayed in the first place. The subtext was a silent, resentful scream.

Joe's temper frayed thin. He brushed his hands back over his hair knowing the gesture would trip every trigger Reston had. He shook his head and sent the braid swinging for the same reason. The muscle-flexing, on the other hand, that was nothing but self-indulgence.

He waited until Reston's revulsion hit maximum before saying, "The worst part is that you believe your own lies. The next worst is how close you came to crushing three lives to preserve Belleview's precious progressive reputation. You're a self-righteous jackass as well as a homophobic hidebound bigot, and I wish I could get away with doing more than making you squirm. Lucky for you I have principles."

Shock. "You can't talk to me that way."

"He can." Kalyani turned the screen towards Reston again, tapped a finger on his desk phone. "And now you will call some reporters and your superiors and set the record straight in time for the funeral. Don't worry, it'll all look shiny-bright in the end. The CSB will get some nice diversity publicity, y'all will get a clean patrol roster here and a rep for integrity too. Everybody wins."

Reston eyed them both as he reached for the phone; looking for the hook, not even realizing that it was set and he was halfway in the boat already. He would figure it out later, when he started wondering why he'd followed their orders now without arguing.

Kalyani wasn't lying; the local unit would benefit from new blood, and exposing the scandal would actually enhance its image once disillusionment over the lies waned. It would also get a new station chief. No laws had been broken, but they'd been bent and twisted. That was only tolerated when it could be denied, no matter how good the intentions were. Reston was about to slit his professional throat by publicly admitting to suppressing facts.

He said, "What do you get out of this?"

Kalyani glanced up at the security monitor. "If we're lucky, we get a neopsych on our roster who believes in the myth of justice for all. Because if enough people like him believe in a myth like that, sometimes it comes true."

4: PRAYERS FOR THE DEPARTED

JOE CHECKED the mirror over the console table, adjusted his suit collar and then watched the pleasantly domestic scene in the room behind him for a few moments.

Carl was pacing barefoot in front of the window while he rolled too-short jacket sleeves to the elbow and made it look like a style choice. Eddie had given up on protesting that his trousers were fine after tripping on them for the fifth time, and Kalyani was taping up the cuffs. She sat on the coffee table with the boy's foot in the lap of her little black dress, leaning forward over her work, and he was on the couch with a throw pillow in his lap and his eyes glued to her breasts.

Kalyani could be a cruel woman.

She had pointed out the previous afternoon that if Carl wasn't going to stand with his family at the funeral then he would be seen as representing Rydder Institute, which she was not about to let him do in travel-rumpled clothes and borrowed ones at that. He'd countered with the valid point that Eddie would be standing with him and didn't have good clothes either. Kalyani accepted the challenge and dragged both of them to one of the little downtown shops.

She'd brought back formal outfits for herself and Joe as well, so they were all going to make a decent showing for the memorial service. Joe wondered what the new CSB captain would say when he found the charges listed on his unit's budget.

A quiet rap at the door preceded Ben opening it and giving the room a cursory check. "Margolis is on his way down," he said.

Seth Margolis had turned out to be a resolutely introverted man who wanted nothing more than to get through this day and leave town. He only cared about the service because he deeply wanted to prove to himself that he wasn't afraid to stay, and he'd accepted the offer to present a united front because he *was* afraid, deeply and justifiably so.

He also spent the previous evening talking with Carl, which had done the both of them a world of good and helped neither of them at all, as was to be expected at this stage. He came inside now with a nod for Joe and a weak smile for other three, and they were on their way a few minutes later.

The funeral was a religious affair held at one of the town's five different denominational churches. The turnout was large, and while snippets of conversation hinted at social storms to come, today the focus was where it should be, on mourning the end of a too-brief life.

Before the service Carl and Eddie met briefly with their family. The discussion was short, respectful and ended with hugs before they beat a retreat to their seats at the rear of the church with Seth, Joe and Kalyani.

Carl frowned at Joe when he found himself under observation. When he reached the pew he said softly, "Do you ever get tired of standing on the outside sneaking looks at other people's insides?"

The taunt slid past Joe's emotional defenses like a knife, sharp and painful. He bit back a hundred valid responses and contented himself with a reproachful stare. *Misery loves company, does it?*

Carl sat down, hunched forward to face the floor, and stayed that way through most of the service.

The interment was announced as family-only. Instead of a general retreat after the service, the congregation went through something like a reception line in reverse. It was a ritual that Joe thought looked like hell on earth for everyone on both sides, and he was glad they were near the front of the queue.

Seth stood silent with a white face and lips pressed tight when he reached Quentin Farley's parents. The father shook his hand: firm grip, no lingering, no words. The silence wasn't disapproval, only emotion tamped down hard. Barely holding on. A lot like Seth.

The mother looked shrunken and drab, gray-faced and red-eyed, but she took Seth's hand and refused to let go until he looked her straight in the eye. "You will stay," she said, and stepped to the side. "He would've wanted that."

Offering Seth a place with the family. Apologizing for not showing him that support before now. Joe felt the stir in the crowd like a cold breeze against the back of his neck. Seth couldn't form an answer aloud. His throat worked, and he shook his head as he let his lover's grieving mother tuck him between herself and her husband.

She stretched out her hand to Carl, next in the line, and when he took it and muttered condolences, she said, "Enough proving you're a big man, you scamp. You will come to the house, after."

It wasn't a question or even an invitation. It was an order trading on a long-standing relationship, and *don't you talk back to me, smartypants*, echoed in it. Carl said somberly, "Yes, Ms. Farley. I'll come. Mom said she dropped off a dish. She should've brought you two. I still eat a lot."

The woman's eyes brimmed with tears, but she managed a trembling smile. "Sassy boy. Eat all you want, only come over the fence one last time. Bring your friends."

Her smile faded, and her voice carried more than the lonely, empty ache of grief. There was *anticipation* in it, and a hint of fear.

Carl tipped his head slightly. "Yes, ma'am. I'll do that."

Joe couldn't filter meaning out the emotional clutter, but he noted that Eddie made a quiet noise somewhere south of a sigh and north of a groan. Once Kalyani had accepted a much more formal invitation and directions to the house for them both, Joe pulled the boy aside. "What's he up to?'"

"Saying good-byes." Eddie stared after his brother, who was hurrying away down the street with Ben in close pursuit. "It's all good." *Wait and see.*

Joe weighed the risks and decided to on trust once again.

JOE AND KALYANI arrived early to the reception, and Joe's earlier puzzlement was resolved when he saw the mother's relief as guest after guest arrived, some with dishes in hand. She had feared silence and shunning in this vulnerable time, but instead there were embraces and tears and sympathy.

Joe sat thigh-to-thigh with Kalyani on a worn and comfortable couch which had been pushed to the wall of the living room to make space for buffets. They sipped at drinks and juggled snacks while conversations and whispered gossip flowed around them. Maintaining social distance took no conscious effort. They were ignored, and the their protection team had made itself conspicuous by its absence. Tasha had remarked, *outside is close enough for this.*

Kalyani nibbled on a carrot stick between swallows of her drink. Finally she sighed. "I know why you never answered Carl's question at the funeral, but are you still thinking about it? I am."

She knew how much it hurt to always be the outsider. The gratitude of clients and the affirmation of peers eased some of the sting for clinicians, but Outreach liaisons were often away from the support of their own. The pain was greater, the sense of dislocation far more severe.

Joe said, "What we do…there are reasons for the secrecy and the security. For remaining Other."

"Please don't get philosophical on me. I haven't finished my third drink." A sip, a nibble. "Somebody needs to climb on the assimilation soapbox again, that's all I'm saying. Isolated populations don't stay healthy long-term. Case in point right here, y'know? Only ever dealing with visiting career psychs and clients and the sticky side of police work —it's warping us all. You know it is."

"The Board's moving ahead on plans for satellite clinics," Joe told her. "You didn't hear it from me, but senior staff got the word in June. Open-door access, using grants and subsidies to support pricing accessible to the general public. Philly, Chicago, Tucson. Omaha or St. Louis. They're vetting real estate. Five years, maybe, and we'll have enough exposure to start accepting minor-issue clients, and then we start out-training clinical neo procedures one at a time to non-Institute students."

She sat quiet for a while, considering possibilities and complications. The unexpected sound of laughter rose nearby, and Joe came to his feet when Eddie came sliding through the crowd like an eel through weeds. He led them to the dining room entrance and stopped there.

Carl sat cross-legged on the floor next to the archway. A standing group had gathered around him, wall to wall to wall. Seth Margolis sat in a chair in the center, looking shell-shocked, worried and more than a little inebriated.

Everyone in the room was young, although most were older than Carl by years. All legal adults, judging by the oh-so-casually hefted and self-consciously held drinks. And all their faces—every one of them—were shining with goodwill.

Then one of the men stepped forward and started talking slow and quiet, sharing an anecdote about Quentin. "My friend," he said, and "I miss him," and Seth's eyes filled with tears.

Carl looked up at Joe, somber and subdued, and Joe met his level stare with a lifted eyebrow that noted his position. On the edge, looking on, not taking part. *Sometimes you have to stay on the outside to make a difference. Yes, it hurts. Yes, it's worth it.*

That smile of Carl's was going to be an incredible tool someday. Now it said *I know* and *I'm sorry* and *thank you* all at once, and Joe nodded his approval.

"I take back what I said about interrogation," Kalyani whispered as they moved discreetly to a corner. "That great big help-the-world-save-itself streak would be wasted on the Feds. Let's steal him for public outreach."

"I'm working on it." Joe squeezed back. "The clinic program we want to start—that's what will make it work, sitting right there. That one and new blood like him."

The scene that followed would have reduced them both

to tears from emotional overload without Eddie's regular laconic interjections. He reduced a young woman in a CAF jumpsuit and buzz cut whose story of water tower vandalism came with sound effects to: "Used to catch frogs with me." The next volunteer, a bearded young man in a black suit, was dismissed with, "Carl stole his Mayfest date two years running."

Then came a couple who didn't look old enough to be as closely attached as their body language and the woman's swollen belly testified. They spun a tale about insults and revenge in the form of rainbow-painted Guernseys that had even Seth giggling by the end. Eddie's *sotto voce* contribution: "Clingy bitch."

Another woman reminisced about a years-long hopeless crush on Quentin and somehow turned bitter into sweet on a joking exchange with Carl. And Eddie said wistfully, "She calls him Squishy. He won't tell me why."

Someone brought in Quentin's parents, and room was made for them, and then other parents and older adults meandered in. Carl kept things moving without pushing, as skillful a job of facilitating as any licensed professional could have managed. He was planting seeds of change the old-fashioned way, with nothing more than heart and hard work. Cauterizing his own severed connections to this community even as he wove Seth into it. *A proper good-bye and a last gift.*

In time the mood started to spin loose and fray towards maudlin, and side conversations sprouted up. Carl took advantage of the distraction to slip out of the room with Eddie behind him. Kalyani put her arm though the crook of Joe's elbow, and after a decent interval they snuck away as well.

The boys were sitting on the kitchen porch in the dark, Eddie on a swing whose chains was being taxed to the squeaking limits, Carl on the top step. They looked at home there.

"When you ran away, when you were five," Joe said, "you ran here."

"Both of us," Carl said. "Mom said I couldn't come to work with her any more unless I stood up for myself. Eddie would hit me when he was hurting inside, and I'd hug him until he felt better. And then Mom said no more studying with the olders or playing with the other littles unless I hit him back. I hated her for being so cruel, so I ran. I wanted to scare her."

"Scared me," Eddie said. *Abandoned.* That thread of fear still remained. "I ran after him."

The cruelty had been unintentional, born of ignorance and misunderstanding. Carl's mother had meant to teach him to defend himself. The adoption papers had been filed less than a year later, so they'd obviously worked through the crisis.

A last piece of the picture resolved into focus for Joe. "Let me guess. Quinn was the one who dragged you both home, and he's the one who taught you how to behave when grownups were watching, so people wouldn't freak out."

"He called us babies," Eddie said. "I punched him."

"You punched everybody," Carl said.

Silence fell, a quiet broken by the continued talking indoors and the chirps of crickets and frogs outside. A rumble came from the rail line to the north. Lights blinked against the stars in the black sky, planes passing far overhead.

Life, moving on.

Eddie stood up and snapped his fingers, and Carl followed him down the steps into the dark without a word. Joe glanced at Kalyani, then took her hand and joined them.

DEDICATIONS

Paul, without you I would be only a dreamer, not an author. Your steadfast support made this happen. No dedication, no acknowledgement, no words will ever be sufficient to express my gratitude and love.

Berni, Blynn, Cathy, Dan, Deb, Doug, Emily, Hugh, John, Lisa, Lynn, Susan, Tess—you are all awesome, and I want the world to know it. At various points in the gestation of this novel, each of you offered critical feedback, monumental editing help, necessary encouragement, or pivotal plotting solutions.
Thank you all.

K. M. Herkes writes and publishes books that dance in the open spaces between science fiction and fantasy, specializing in stories about damaged souls, complicated lives, and triumphs of the spirit.

Professional development started with a Bachelor of Science degree in Biology and now includes experience in classroom teaching, animal training, aquaculture, horticulture, bookselling, and retail operations. Personal development is ongoing. Cats are involved.

When she isn't writing, she works at the Mount Prospect Public Library. She also digs holes in her backyard for fun, enjoys experimental baking, and wrangles butterflies.

Visit dawnrigger.com and check out extras like free short stories, story-inspired artwork, links to the author's media, and blog rants on life, the universe, and writing. While you're there, sign up for rare Dawnrigger Publishing email alerts and get a subscriber-exclusive free short story .